KIT'S
HOME RUN

KIT • 1934

BY VALERIE TRIPP

ILLUSTRATIONS WALTER RANE

VIGNETTES PHILIP HOOD, SUSAN MCALILEY

THE AMERICAN GIRLS COLLECTION®

Published by Pleasant Company Publications
For information, address: Book Editor, Pleasant Company Publications,
8400 Fairway Place, P.O. Box 620998, Middleton, WI 53562.

Visit our Web site at **americangirl.com**

Printed in Singapore.
02 03 04 05 06 07 08 09 TWP 10 9 8 7 6 5 4 3 2 1

Library of Congress Cataloging-in-Publication Data

Tripp, Valerie, 1951–
Kit's home run / by Valerie Tripp ;
illustrations by Walter Rane ; vignettes, Philip Hood, Susan McAliley.
p. cm. — (The American girls collection)
Summary: In 1933 Cincinnati, Kit is an enthusiastic baseball player
whose home run slide has surprising consequences. Includes historical notes
on major league baseball and the Cincinnati Reds in the 1930s and provides
ideas for decorating a baseball cap.
ISBN 1-58485-482-0
[1. Baseball—Fiction. 2. Prejudices—Fiction.
3. Depressions—1929—Fiction. 4. Cincinnati (Ohio)—Fiction.]
I. Rane, Walter, ill. II. Hood, Philip, ill. III. McAliley, Susan, ill. IV. Title. V. Series.
PZ7.T7363 Ki 2002 [Fic]—dc21 2001036647

The
**AMERICAN GIRLS
COLLECTION**™

OTHER AMERICAN GIRLS
SHORT STORIES:

FELICITY DISCOVERS A SECRET

JUST JOSEFINA

KIRSTEN AND THE CHIPPEWA

ADDY STUDIES FREEDOM

SAMANTHA'S BLUE BICYCLE

MOLLY'S A+ PARTNER

PICTURE CREDITS

The following individuals and organizations have generously given permission to reprint illustrations contained in "Looking Back": p. 38—Baseball Hall of Fame Library, Cooperstown, NY; p. 39—Minnesota Historical Society; p. 40—Franklin D. Roosevelt Library; p. 41—David M. Spindel; p. 43—© Schenectady Museum, Hall of Electrical History Foundation/CORBIS; p. 44—Walter Lanier "Red" Barber Collection, University Archives, Department of Special Collections, George A. Smathers Libraries, University of Florida; p. 45—Bettmann/CORBIS; p. 46—David M. Spindel; p. 47—National Baseball Hall of Fame Library, Cooperstown, NY; p. 48—Photography by Jamie Young and craft by June Pratt.

TABLE OF CONTENTS

KIT'S FAMILY

DAD
Kit's father, a businessman facing the problems of the Great Depression.

MOTHER
Kit's mother, who takes care of her family and their home with strength and determination.

KIT
A clever, resourceful girl who helps her family cope with the dark days of the Depression.

CHARLIE
Kit's affectionate and supportive older brother.

AUNT MILLIE
The lively and loving woman who raised Dad.

MRS. HOWARD

*Mother's garden club
friend, who is a guest
in the Kittredge home.*

STIRLING
HOWARD

*Mrs. Howard's son,
whose delicate health hides
surprising strengths.*

KIT'S
HOME RUN

On a hot June afternoon, Kit Kittredge was in her backyard taking a break from her chores and playing catch with her friend Stirling Howard. Kit's dog, Grace, was there too, snoozing. School was out, the sky was blue, and it was baseball season. Stirling fired a fastball to Kit. It landed solidly in her mitt with a *thonk!* Kit grinned. She loved that sound. She even liked how Stirling's fastball stung her hand through the mitt and made it tingle.

"For a skinny guy, you've got a pretty good arm," Kit said to Stirling as she tossed the ball back to him.

Stirling made the catch, then kiddingly flexed his arm to make a muscle. "It's from carrying all those newspapers," he said. Stirling had surprised everyone by going out the very first day of summer vacation and finding himself a job selling newspapers on a street corner. He shot the ball back to Kit, who caught it with ease. "And you're a pretty good catcher— almost as good as Ernie Lombardi!" he joshed.

Ernie Lombardi was the catcher and Kit's favorite player on the Cincinnati Reds baseball team. "Wouldn't it be great to go

to Redland Field and see
Ernie play?" Kit asked.

"It sure would," agreed
Stirling. Ernie was his favorite
player, too.

Redland Field

Kit knew Stirling was thinking the
same thing she was. Going to a Reds'
game was about as likely as going to the
moon. Kit's dad had lost his job almost a
year ago because of the Depression. Her
family had to watch every penny. They
certainly did not have money to spend
on tickets to a baseball game! They would
have lost their *house* if they hadn't been
rescued by Dad's Aunt Millie, who had
used her own money to pay the bank
what they owed on the mortgage.

The situation that Stirling and his mother were in was even worse. Mr. Howard was gone. Stirling and Mrs. Howard lived in the Kittredges' house as boarders, but they hadn't been able to pay any rent for months. The money Stirling made selling newspapers was their only income.

Kit sent the ball back to Stirling. "Dad and I went to a Reds' game last year," she said. She didn't have to add, "Before Dad lost his job." How well Kit remembered every detail of that day at the game: the cheers of the crowd and the crack of the bats smacking the balls, the green of the field, the heat of the sun,

4

and the taste and the smell of the mustardy hot dogs. "We saw Ernie hit a home run," Kit said to Stirling. "What a hit! And good old Ernie just sort of strolled around the bases. He ran so slowly that he had to dive headfirst into home plate to beat the ball! He almost slowpoked himself out of the run." Kit chuckled. "Ernie's a great catcher and a great slugger," she said. "But he sure is a slow runner."

"Well," said Stirling as he tossed a low slider to Kit, "no one's good at *everything*. That's the idea of a team. Everybody does something different to help the team win, right?"

"Right," said Kit. She threw a

grounder, which Stirling scooped up smoothly. "But—"

"Stirling, dear," a voice interrupted. It was Mrs. Howard, calling as she came fluttering out of the house. Grace looked up, ever hopeful of a snack. But Mrs. Howard brought only nervous flurry with her.

"It's time for you to go sell your papers," Mrs. Howard said to Stirling. "I don't want you to rush or you'll get overheated."

"Yes, Mother," said Stirling.

"Go inside and wash your hands, lamby," said Mrs. Howard. "And don't forget to wear your cap. Too much sun is not good for your fair skin."

"Yes, Mother," said Stirling. He
turned to Kit. "Bye," he said. He shot one
last blaster to her, high into the sky.

"Bye," said Kit. She squinted into
the sun. Keeping her eye on the ball, Kit
took one step back, then another. Without
looking behind her, Kit ran backward.
She stretched out her arm, took a wild
leap, and snagged the ball in mid-air.
"Got it!" she shouted. Suddenly, *bam!* Kit
slammed into a rose trellis and knocked
it over so that it crashed to the ground.
Kit landed on top of the trellis, sitting
down hard on the thorny roses.

Mrs. Howard and Stirling hurried to
her. "Kit!" Mrs. Howard cried. "Are you
all right?"

"Sure," said Kit, even though her arms were rather pricked and scratched.

"Oh, but my roses," Mrs. Howard wailed. She sank to her knees next to the squashed blossoms and scattered leaves and petals. "You've *killed* them."

Kit stood up. She and Stirling looked at the ruined roses. Then they looked at each other and whispered, "Uh-oh."

The trellis roses were Mrs. Howard's particular pets. The plants had been limp and lifeless until she started nursing them along. She'd watered and pruned them. She'd draped blankets over them when the temperature was too cool. She'd cooed to them as if they were babies and coaxed them into blooming beautifully. And now, thanks to Kit's catch, they were flattened.

"Gosh, Mrs. Howard," said Kit, surveying the damage. "I'm sorry."

"Me, too," said Stirling. "Sorry, Mother."

"It's that baseball playing!" said Mrs. Howard as she fussed with the crushed roses. "You know I don't like it, Stirling. Your bones are delicate, and I worry that you'll be hurt." She shook her head helplessly. "And now it has hurt my roses." Mrs. Howard sighed. "But, Stirling, you had better go to your job," she said. "It won't do to be late."

"Yes, Mother," said Stirling. He left, sending Kit a sympathetic glance over his shoulder.

"Want me to help you fix the trellis?" Kit asked Mrs. Howard.

"No," said Mrs. Howard. She looked up. "Really, Kit, I must say I do not understand why you like baseball. It's so rough and noisy. In my day, girls were graceful and gentle and quiet. Not tomboys! Just look at you now, all dirty and sweaty." Mrs. Howard shuddered, as if Kit's appearance pained her. "Don't you want to go inside and clean yourself up?"

"Yes, ma'am," said Kit.

That was all Kit said. But it was certainly not all she was thinking as she went into the house, with Grace trailing along behind her. Kit was very sorry she had ruined the roses—truly she was. *But Mrs. Howard didn't have to make such a fuss about it*, Kit thought. She scrubbed her scratched and grimy hands and then scoured out the sink. *Mrs. Howard makes a fuss about everything—flowers, cleanliness, baseball, Stirling.*

And it was all so pointless! Take

Stirling. Mrs. Howard fretted over him
as if he were still the pitiful weakling he
had been when they came to live at the
Kittredges'. But he wasn't! He still looked
a bit like a pip-squeak, but he was healthy
and sturdy. He even had a real job and
made a useful contribution to the house-
hold, which was more than anyone could
say for Mrs. Howard these days. She used
to do her fair share of the housework. But
Aunt Millie had taken that over. Now all
Mrs. Howard did was volunteer at the
hospital, weeding and watering the flower
beds there. At home, she insisted on
cleaning the room that she and Stirling
lived in. She washed their sheets and
clothing herself. Kit figured that was

because she was so persnickety that no one could do it well enough to suit her.

Mother has said a hundred times that we've all got to work together to make our boarding house succeed, Kit said to herself as she went back to her afternoon chores. *If we're a team, Mrs. Howard sure isn't a star player.*

❦

"Run, Kit, run!" someone yelled.

Kit poured on the speed and rounded second base. Out of the corner of her eye, she saw the left fielder chasing the ball as it bounced across the grass. Kit had been on her way home from the library when some

13

friends had asked her to join their baseball
game. Now she was on her way to home
plate after socking a powerful grounder
to left field. The bases were loaded, so
Kit's hit had already brought three other
runners home. If Kit beat the ball back to
the catcher, her hit would not only be a
home run, it would be a grand slam.

"Keep going, Kit!" her teammates
hollered as she passed third base, run-
ning flat out.

But oh, no! Kit saw the ball speeding
through the air. The catcher stepped
forward, mitt raised, to catch it and tag
Kit out. There was only one thing to do.
Dive, Kit said to herself, *Dive like Ernie
Lombardi.*

Kit dove. Flinging her arms forward, she flew through the air toward home. She landed with an *oomph!* and slid on her stomach with her arms outstretched, trying to touch home plate before the catcher caught the ball. He jumped up, and just as Kit hit the plate, he snagged the ball and twisted around to tag her. *Pow!* His elbow smacked Kit right in the kisser. But Kit didn't care. She was safe! Her face might've been clobbered, but so was the other team. Her grand slam had scored four runs! Her team won, thanks to Kit's home run.

"Hurray!" her team cheered, rushing to the field. Kit stood up gingerly and brushed the dirt from her dress. Her

*Kit landed with an **oomph!***

teammates thumped her on the back
to congratulate her. She turned and
grinned. *Ouch!* Grinning made her lip
sting.

Suddenly, everyone was quiet.

"Yikes," said the catcher. "Sorry."

"What's the matter?" Kit asked. But
her mouth was so mushy, it sounded like
"Wassamada?"

"Your lip," said the catcher.

Kit gently prodded her lip with her
tongue and tasted blood. She touched
her lip with her finger, and it came away
bloody. Kit looked down. The front of her
dress was smeared with dust and blood.

"I bet your lip is going to need
stitches," a boy said, impressed.

"Probably later you'll have a black eye, too," another added eagerly.

"You'd better go home," said a girl on Kit's team.

"Yeah," Kit said. She wobbled her way to the edge of the field and picked up her library books. "Bye."

"It was a great slide, though," the girl called after her. "Thanks, Kit!"

Kit felt weak and muzzy-headed as she walked home, holding her hankie against her bloody mouth. *Mother and Aunt Millie will know what to do,* she comforted herself. Then Kit came to a dead stop. *Oh, no!* she remembered. Mother, Dad, and Aunt Millie weren't home. They had gone to the bank to find out about getting a Homeowner's Loan so that they could continue to pay the mortgage. The boarders were at work or gone. Stirling was on his corner downtown selling newspapers. The only person at home was Mrs. I-don't-approve-of-baseball, Mrs. Fussbudget, Stirling's mother. Kit groaned to herself, *Wait till she gets a load of my face. She'll have a fit! And after that, she'll have a lot of disapproving things to say about baseball—and me.*

Kit dragged her feet, but she couldn't help getting home eventually.

As she put her books on the hall table, she heard Mrs. Howard puttering in the kitchen, so she pushed open the swinging door. Mrs. Howard turned from the sink. Her eyes widened.

"Kit!" Mrs. Howard said. "Your face! How did that happen? Oh! Don't tell me. You were playing baseball."

Kit nodded yes. She steeled herself for the anti–tomboy and baseball fussing she was sure would come. She was also sure the fussing would be more bother-some than the injuries themselves, which, by the way, were beginning to hurt badly.

But instead Mrs. Howard put her arm around Kit's shoulders and steered her to a chair. "Sit down, lamby," she said sympathetically.

Kit sat. Mrs. Howard went into action. She knew just what to do. She washed Kit's injuries carefully, murmuring reassurances all the while. She gave Kit a cool, wet dishcloth to hold to her lip and eye, which made them hurt less. She brought Kit fresh clothes and put her dirty, sweaty, bloodstained dress in cold water to soak. She was patient and gentle, calm and kind.

After Kit changed, Mrs. Howard asked, "Feel a little better now, dear?"

Kit nodded yes again. "Sanks," she said.

Mrs. Howard examined Kit's eye and lip. "We'd better go to the hospital," she said. "A doctor should look at your eye. And I think your lip needs stitches." She patted Kit's hand. "I'm afraid I have

21

no money for a cab. Do you feel up to
walking?"

Kit nodded yes a third time. She
stood up and weaved a little bit.

"You're a brave girl," Mrs. Howard
said. "Lean on me."

The walk to the hospital was not
long, but Kit was very grateful for
Mrs. Howard's arm. She felt rather
woozy in the heat and bright sunshine.
Mrs. Howard didn't rush. She walked
slowly and spoke soft encouragements
every step of the way, as if Kit were a
baby learning to toddle. Normally, of
course, Kit hated being treated like a
baby. But right now, she liked it. *Mrs.
Howard is a pretty good person to be with*

when you're hurt, Kit thought. *Fussy babying feels nice when you're on the way to the hospital for stitches.*

"Sanks," said Kit, struggling to speak with her sore, swollen lip. "Sanks for being so nice."

"Well," said Mrs. Howard with a small smile, "taking care of injured things like people and plants is all I'm good at besides cooking and cleaning. I'm actually grateful to you, dear, for giving me a chance to feel useful for a change. Stirling doesn't need me to fuss over him the way he used to, and now that Aunt Millie is here, well . . ." Mrs. Howard sighed.

"But—" Kit began.

"Don't try to talk, dear," said

23

Mrs. Howard. "It'll hurt your poor lip."

Kit pressed the dishcloth back against her lip and stopped talking. But she didn't stop talking about Mrs. Howard. *I guess I needed a clonk on the head to finally understand her*, Kit thought.

When they reached the hospital, Mrs. Howard marched right up to the nurse at the admitting desk. Kit stood quietly, water droplets polka-dotting the front of her dress, while Mrs. Howard arranged for her to be seen as soon as a doctor was free. While they waited,

Mrs. Howard led Kit to a small hospitality shop just off the front lobby.

"There's a sink in this

shop," Mrs. Howard explained to Kit. "I use it to wash my hands when I come here to tend the flower beds. We'll rinse out your dishcloth at the sink."

"All right," said Kit. She could talk a little better now. Her lip didn't hurt quite so much, and the bleeding had stopped.

The hospitality shop was busy. People were buying magazines, cards, candy, flowers, and potted plants to give to the patients they'd come to visit in the hospital. Every seat at the lunch counter was taken. Mrs. Howard called out to the man in charge, "Mr. Hoffstader, we're going to use the sink, if we may."

"Go ahead, ma'am," he replied with a smile.

Mrs. Howard led the way to the sink. She took the dishcloth and rinsed it out over the drain. When she noticed some very thirsty-looking potted plants on the counter nearby, she wrung out the dishcloth over the top of them.

Mrs. Howard sure does like pitiful plants, thought Kit as she watched.

Mr. Hoffstader was watching, too. After he served some hamburgers, he began to slap together some egg-salad sandwiches. He said to Mrs. Howard, "You're one of the garden club ladies, aren't you?"

"Why, yes," said Mrs. Howard.

"I've seen you weeding and watering the plants outside the hospital," said

Mr. Hoffstader. "You come more often than the other ladies."

"Why, yes, I guess so," said Mrs. Howard.

"She loves plants," Kit piped up. Then suddenly, Kit had one of the best brainstorms she had ever had in her life. "Mr. Hoffstader," she asked, "who takes care of the plants and flowers here in your shop?"

"My wife used to," Mr. Hoffstader answered, up to his elbows in egg salad, "but she's been home with our new baby for two weeks now. I'm usually too busy cooking or cleaning up to remember the plants."

Kit felt the same way she'd felt in the

baseball game. She was just going to
have to dive headfirst and hope for the
best. "Seems like you could use a helper,"
she said, taking the plunge. "Mrs. Howard
would be perfect. She's not only great
with plants. She's also great at cleaning,
and she's a good cook, too. She's very
nice to injured people, so everyone
would like her here at the hospital." Kit
turned to Mrs. Howard and asked, "Isn't
that true?"

Mrs. Howard blushed. "Why, yes,
I guess so," she said.

 Mr. Hoffstader paused on
his way to the cash register. "I
do need help during the lunch
hour," he said. "But I couldn't

afford to pay much. Would two dollars a week be all right?"

Mrs. Howard was too surprised to talk. Kit gave her a gentle nudge. "Why, yes, I guess so," Mrs. Howard finally said.

"Can you start tomorrow?" asked Mr. Hoffstader.

"Why, yes, I . . ." Mrs. Howard

29

began again. Then she stopped herself. She beamed at Kit, then said firmly to Mr. Hoffstader, "Yes, I am sure I can!"

"See you tomorrow then," said Mr. Hoffstader. "Eleven o'clock?"

"Eleven o'clock," Mrs. Howard repeated as she and Kit left to go back to the waiting room. "Good-bye. And thank you!"

Mrs. Howard sat down on one of the waiting-room chairs. "Kit," she asked, "did that really happen? Did you just find me a job?"

Kit smiled a crooked smile. "Why, yes, I guess so," she said.

Mrs. Howard laughed. "How lucky that you got a black eye and a split lip," she said. "I'll never fuss at you or Stirling about baseball again."

❧

Mrs. Howard kept her word. She didn't fuss about baseball. She didn't fuss about *anything* at home nearly as much as she used to. Stirling said it was because she was happy because she could finally pay Kit's parents some rent. But Kit thought Mrs. Howard didn't fuss at home because she used up her fussiness at work, where it was appreciated. Mr. Hoffstader was very pleased with her, Mrs. Howard had admitted. She was the best cleaner he'd ever seen, and the plants and flowers had never been cared for so well.

"Kit found the perfect job for me," Mrs. Howard often said.

After Mrs. Howard had been working for several weeks, she found the perfect

way to thank Kit for her perfect job. She took Kit and Stirling to a Reds' game on Ladies' Day!

"It's very nice of you to do this," Kit said to her as they took their seats. Kit knew very, very well that baseball was not Mrs. Howard's sort of thing at all. And as the game went on, Kit could tell that Mrs. Howard did not have the faintest idea what was happening, though she tried to follow the plays.

It was a terrific game. At the bottom of the seventh inning, Ernie Lombardi smacked a homer over center field, and the crowd went wild. Everyone jumped up and cheered—except poor, puzzled Mrs. Howard.

"What's happening?" she asked Kit above the hubbub.

Kit had to shout. "Ernie Lombardi hit a home run!" she explained. "And the bases were loaded, so it's a grand slam. That means his home run will bring in four runs for the team."

"Oh," said Mrs. Howard brightly.

Kit thought she did not understand. But later, on the way home, Mrs. Howard said, "Mr. Lombardi's home run was like

Kit had to shout. "Ernie Lombardi hit a home run!"

yours, Kit. Because of it, four good things happened. I got a job, Stirling doesn't have me fussing over him so much, your parents have my rent coming in, and—"

"—and I got to come to a Reds' game!" Kit finished for her.

"Yes!" said Mrs. Howard. "Your home run was *truly* a grand slam."

VALERIE TRIPP

At 9 Now

When I was Kit's age, I liked to play baseball in the front yard with my brother, Granger. Once I got a black eye in a game, just like Kit did. But I never hit a grand slam!

Valerie Tripp has written forty-four books in The American Girls Collection, including seven about Kit.

A PEEK INTO
THE PAST

Major-league baseball was an exciting sport for fans to follow during the Great Depression. Many of baseball's greatest stars, like Babe Ruth, Lou Gehrig, and Joe DiMaggio, played during the 1930s. At a time when newspapers were filled with dark news of the Depression, fans eagerly turned to the sports page to read about their favorite teams. Kids followed the sport, too, by collecting

Baseball cards like these came with card-sized sheets of bubble gum.

baseball cards with portraits of the players they loved.

At the same time, a national movement was under way to encourage people of all ages to play sports at school and in the community. Leaders of the movement believed that organized sports would help people forget their troubles and would help unemployed people fill their free time.

Kids played "kittenball," later known as softball.

President Roosevelt himself strongly supported baseball. Under the Works

Roosevelt tossed out the first ball in game three of the 1933 World Series.

Progress Administration (WPA), which created many jobs during the Depression, the government built thousands of baseball diamonds and other sports fields across the country.

Though many people were playing baseball and following news about professional teams, few people could afford to attend major-league games during the

Depression. Because of low attendance at games, many teams went bankrupt or had to sell their best players to other teams, which hurt attendance even more.

The Cincinnati Reds, Kit's favorite team, were struggling more than most teams

Cincinnati Reds souvenirs

because the Reds had a bad record. In 1934, they were the worst team in the National League. The owner of the Reds went bankrupt, and the team was purchased by Powel Crosley Jr., a Cincinnati businessman. Crosley and the team manager, Larry MacPhail, needed to take drastic steps to turn the team around.

In 1935, MacPhail tried something that changed major-league baseball forever—he held seven games at night. Midweek games usually started at 3:00 P.M., but many people couldn't attend because they worked until 5:00. The Reds' first night game, on May 24, 1935, was a great success. MacPhail asked President Roosevelt to turn on the 632 lights around the field by flipping a remote-control switch in the White House hundreds of miles away! As many as 18,000 fans attended that first night game, and by the sixth night game, attendance was estimated at over 35,000. Fights broke out over seats, and those who couldn't sit lined the playing field.

More fans could attend games that were held at night.
The increase in ticket sales helped the Reds stay in business.

Another way that the Reds increased fan support was by broadcasting some of their games over the radio. Radio was free advertising that reached for hundreds of miles. Soon, people were following the Reds from as far away as Kentucky, Indiana, and West Virginia. And faraway fans began traveling to the park that was by now known as Crosley Field to see the Reds up close. Nothing drew fans, though, like sheer talent. The Reds had one of

Red Barber broadcast Reds' games over the radio from 1934 until 1938.

baseball's top catchers in the 1930s—Ernie Lombardi, known as the "Schnozz" because of his large nose. Ernie was also famous for his long, hard hits. He had

Ernie Lombardi

consistently high batting averages and was the only catcher to win two National League batting titles. In 1938, he also won the league's Most Valuable Player award. Everybody loved him—teammates, opponents, and especially fans. In 1939, Ernie helped the Reds win their first pennant in 20 years. And in 1940, they

Fans showed support by wearing little ballplayer pins.

won the World Series against the Detroit Tigers. It looked as if the Reds had finally turned things around.

Unfortunately, World War Two was about to hit. In the early 1940s, most professional baseball players went off to war. To keep the sport alive, women formed their own league—the All-American Girls Professional Baseball League. Hundreds of female players tried out for the league. Kit, who would have been a young woman by this time, might have been one of them! The players who were selected were soon playing games for packed stands. Thanks to the spirit and talent of these women, fans on the home front would continue to turn to baseball to help them forget their troubles.

Players trained all day and then played games at night—six nights a week.

PERSONALIZE
A BASEBALL CAP

*Top off your style with a cap made
just for you.*

Kit would have needed a baseball
cap to shield her eyes during pick-up
baseball games in the park. With some
of Aunt Millie's fabric scraps and a few
odds and ends from around the house,
Kit might have created a cap as unique
as her own fun-loving personality.

Use odds and ends to create your
own sporty cap. If sports aren't your
style, try bright blossoms, colorful
shapes, or anything else that says "you."

YOU WILL NEED:

Paper and a pencil
Scissors
Straight pins
Fabric scraps
A plain baseball cap
A needle and thread
Embroidery floss
Buttons

Creating an Appliqué

Use fabric scraps to create your own appliqués, just as Kit might have done.

1. Use the pencil to draw a pattern on the paper. Cut out the pattern.

2. Pin the pattern to a fabric scrap, and cut around the pattern. Position the cutout on your cap, avoiding seams.

3. Thread a needle with 2 strands of embroidery floss. Starting inside the cap, bring the needle up beside the edge of the cutout.

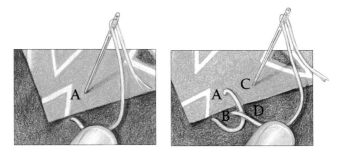

4. Holding the thread down with your thumb, go down at A. Come up at B, bringing the needle *over* the thread held by the thumb. Go down at C, and come up again at D. Keep going until you've sewn around all edges of the cutout.

5. Knot your thread close to your last stitch on the inside of the cap. Cut off the extra thread.

Sewing On a Button

Dot and decorate your cap with buttons of different shapes, sizes, and colors.

1. To sew on a button, pull thread through the eye of a needle until the ends of the thread are even. Knot them together.

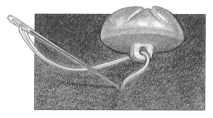

2. To sew on a shank button: Come up through both the fabric and the loop, then go back down. Repeat 3 times.

To sew on a 2-hole button: Come up through one hole and go down through the other. Repeat 3 times.

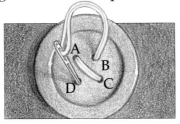

To sew on a 4-hole button: Come up at A and go down at C. Repeat 3 times. Come up at B and go down at D. Repeat 3 times.

3. Knot your thread inside the cap when finished. Cut off the extra thread.

Need More Ideas?

- Look for fun sew-on or iron-on appliqués at fabric stores.

- Create iron-on appliqués using *fusable web,* or iron-on material, found at fabric stores.

- Autograph your cap using fabric paint or fabric markers.

- Use fabric glue to add rickrack or ribbon.

- Sew on dangling decorations such as charms or beads.

American Girl ®

PO BOX 620497
MIDDLETON WI 53562-0497

American Girl®
Catalogue Request

Join our mailing list! Just drop this card
in the mail, call **1-800-845-0005**, or visit
our Web site at **americangirl.com**.

Send me a catalogue

Send my friend a catalogue:

Due to a printing error, this card
does not meet postal regulations.

To receive your FREE
American Girl® catalogue,
please call 1-800-845-0005.

Name _____

Address _____

City _____ State _____ Zip 1225i

Girl's birth date: _____ / _____
       month

Parent's signature _____